Angel the Pig

story and pictures by Arnold Clapman

SILVER PRESS
Parsippany, New Jersey

Published by Silver Press,
an imprint of Silver Burdett Press,
A Paramount Communications Company
299 Jefferson Road
Parsippany, NJ 07054
Printed in Mexico

10 9 8 7 6 5 4 3 2 1

Library of Congress Cataloging-in-Publication Data
Clapman, Arnold.
Angel the pig/by Arnold Clapman: illustrated by
Arnold Clapman. p. cm.
Summary: Although she longs to be like the others,
a small pig can't help being an individual.
[1. Pigs—Fiction. 2. Individuality—Fiction.]
PZ7.C52924Ang 1995
[E]—dc20 94-20302 CIP AC

ISBN 0-382-24662-4 (S/C)

Angel the pig was very small.

But she wanted to be big and fat like the others.

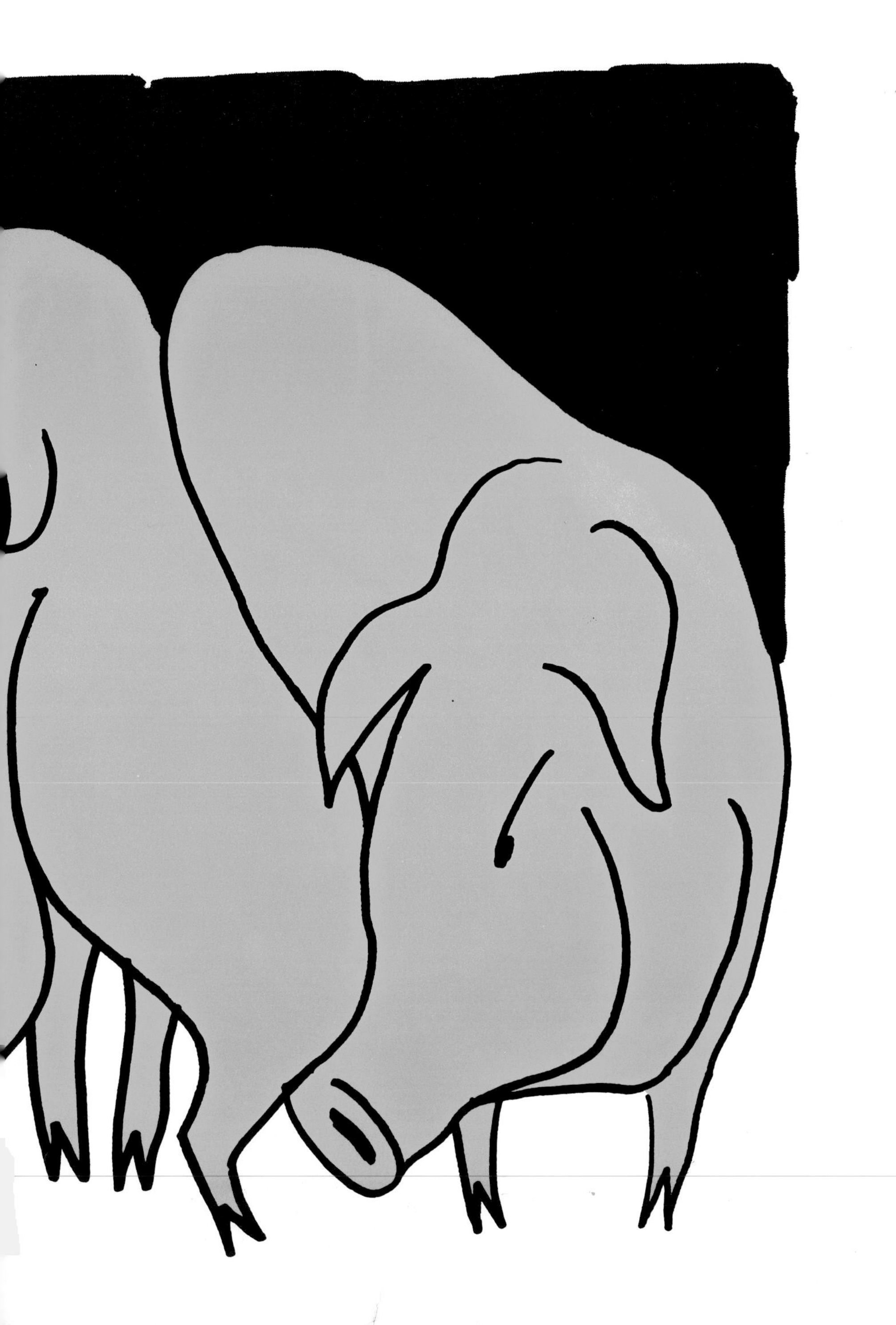

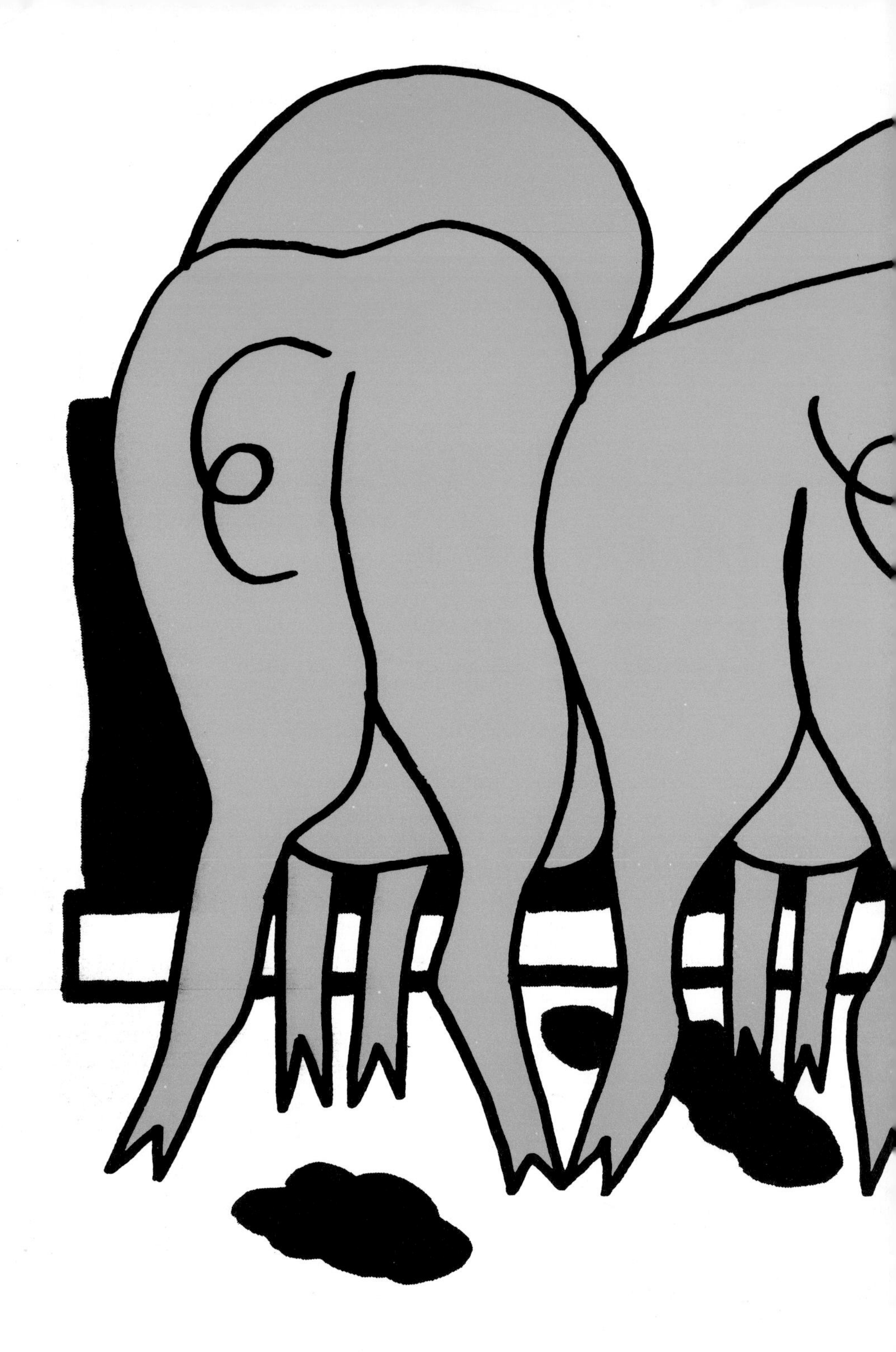

She ate with the others.

She went to sleep with the others.

She grunted with the others too.

But she was not like the others.

Angel did not like to rest.

She liked to play a lot,

And do new things.

One day Angel asked the other pigs, "How can I be like you?"

"You could sit in the mud more," grunted one.

"Eat and sleep more," grunted another.

"Why don't you just sit around and be a pig?" grunted the others.

NT

Angel did just that.

Now she is like the others,

But only sometimes.